ORCHESTRANIMALS

Vlasta van Kampen ♪ Irene C. Eugen

Scholastic Inc.

New York   Toronto   London   Auckland   Sydney

For my parents, Frank and Muriel.
Vlasta

For my loving grandmother, Cornelia.
Irene

And for Jean Eugen, whose vision of the orchestra
inspired this project.
Vlasta and Irene

ISBN 0-590-43151-X

Text copyright © 1989 by Vlasta van Kampen, Irene C. Eugen
and Scholastic Tab Publications Ltd.
Illustrations copyright © 1989 by Vlasta van Kampen.
Music copyright © 1989 by Irene C. Eugen.
All rights reserved. Published by Scholastic Inc.
by arrangement with Scholastic Tab Publications, Ltd.

12 11 10 9 8 7 6 5 4 3 2 1   6   0 1 2 3 4 5/9

Printed in the U.S.A.   08

"Where is everyone?"
muttered the conductor.

"Only ten minutes!
I need players to bow,
players to blow,
and players to hit to the beat . . .
And where's Crash?"

"I don't know, but I'm here,"
said the octopus, sliding a perfect
scale across the keyboard.

"I'm here," said the fox.
"I had trouble putting my new flute together
till I remembered the trick."
He waved his flute and sang:
"The head joint's connected to the body joint . . .
the body joint's connected to the foot joint . . ."

6

"Enough," snapped the conductor.

head joint

body joint

foot joint

"I'm here," said the flamingo.
Her beak was even blacker
than usual.
"I couldn't find my clarinet.
It was mixed in with my
children's licorice sticks."

also called
licorice stick

"I'm here," hiccupped the pelican.

"So I see. What's *your* excuse?"

"I was playing some high piccolo trills
at the seashore when fish started jumping.
Hundreds of them.
I just couldn't let a good meal go by!"

trills are 2 repeated notes played rapidly

cane reed is made
into a mouthpiece

"I'm here," said the duck.
Behind him he dragged a bundle of long wet reeds.
"I found these in the pond. I'm going to use one
for my oboe."

"I'm here," lisped the anteater,
tugging at his bassoon. "Oh, rats!" he sniveled.
"First I practice till my tongue gets stuck,
then I stub my toe on these wretched reeds!"

The conductor groaned and kicked the reeds
under a chair.

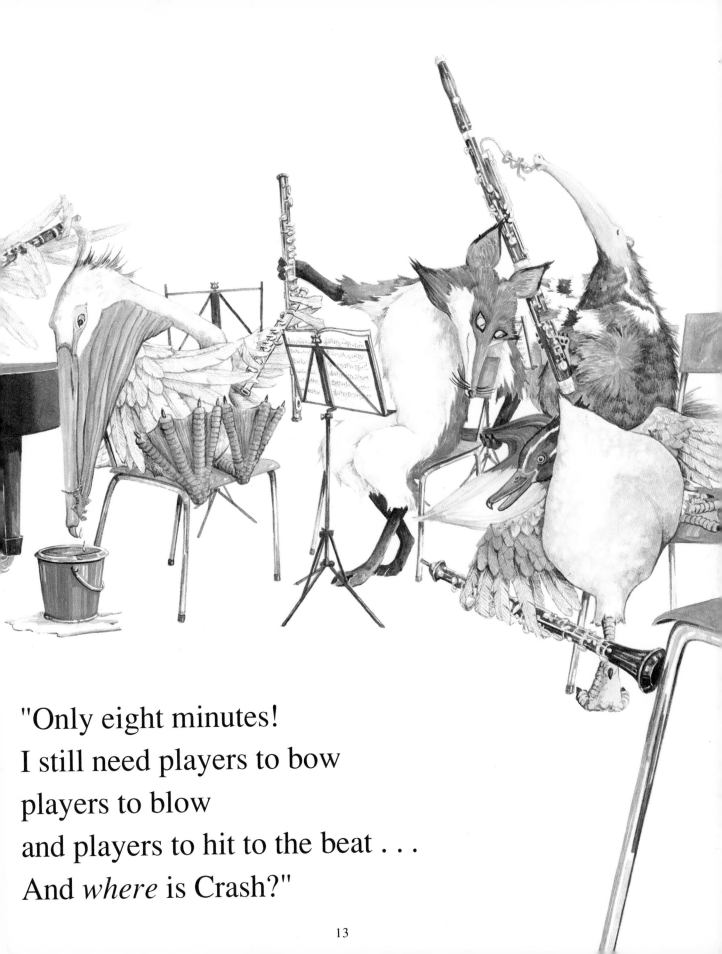

"Only eight minutes!
I still need players to bow
players to blow
and players to hit to the beat . . .
And *where* is Crash?"

"I don't know, but I'm here," said the beaver.
"I got hungry and chewed on my violin.
I fiddled with it but couldn't fix it,
so I had to find a new one."

tuning peg

chin rest

"I'm here," said the raccoon.
He had his viola tucked under his arm.

"About time too! Why are you so late?"

"My bow needed new
hairs," he explained,
"but I had trouble finding
a horse with a long
enough tail."

horsehair is used
to make a bow

"I'm here," said the kangaroo,
planting her cello peg a little too firmly on the stage.
"I couldn't get a babysitter . . . again."

peg holds cello upright

double bass is the
largest stringed instrument

"We're here," said the alligator twins.

"My turn to pizz tonight," said one.

"No, mine," said the other. "It's your turn to bow."

Their identical snouts challenged each other across the double bass.

"Stop that bickering!" shouted the conductor.

He raised his eyes to the ceiling.
"Only five minutes!
I have players to bow,
but need players to blow
and players to hit to the beat . . .
And where is *Crash*?"

"I don't know, but I'm here,"
said the elephant.
She sneezed a mighty sneeze.
"This hayfever is terrible.
I don't know if I can play tonight."

"Not play? You *have* to play! Try!"

The blast she gave on her trumpet
made the rafters ring.

trombone slide is
moved in and out

"I'm here," said the pig.
"Oops! Sorry, maestro! I fell into the slop
trough and didn't have time to clean up.
My trombone slide is slippery."

"I'm here," said the bear.
"Went honey hunting. Found a hive. Trapped
the bees in my French horn. Nozzle's sore . . .
But, oh, will my notes buzz sweet tonight!"

"I'm here," puffed the hippo.

"I don't know what's wrong with this tuba. I can't get a note out of it."

"More problems!" the conductor moaned. "It's almost time to begin and you're still not all here!"

"Only two minutes!
I have players to bow
and players to blow,
but no players to hit to the beat . . .
And where is Crash?"

"I don't know, but I'm here,"
said the bat,
plucking at the harp strings.

"Who are you?
Where's my harpist?"

"He couldn't make it.
But don't worry.
I'm an expert. I'll wing it.

tuning pedals

"I'm here," said the lion.

He grinned and waved his drumsticks.

"A friend borrowed my sticks to clean his ears.

Talk about wax! Had to stop and buy new ones . . .

Hey, where's Crash?"

concertmaster is the first violin and tunes the orchestra by playing the note "A"

"I wish I knew!" exploded the conductor.
He hurried backstage to take one last look.
How could Crash miss his special performance?

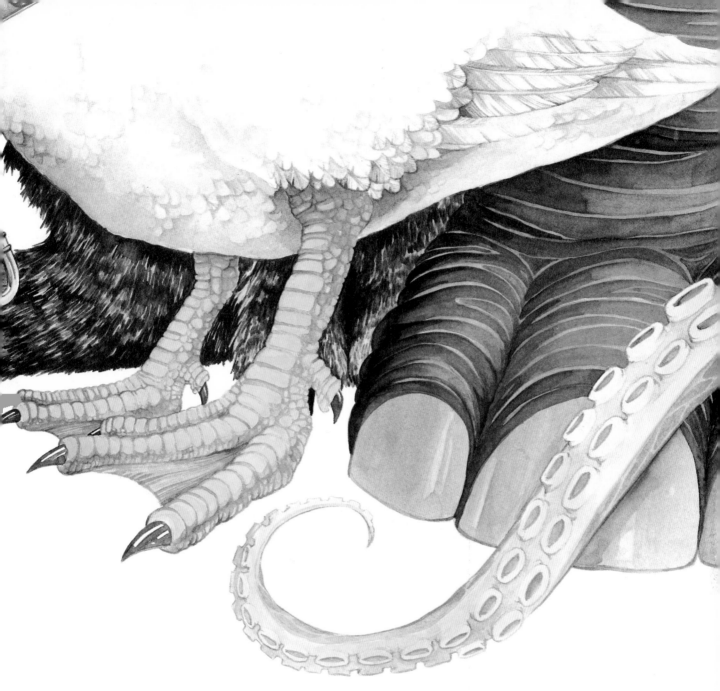

The lights dimmed. The curtains opened.
Applause broke out as the concertmaster
picked up his bow and stepped forward.
The musicians tuned their instruments.
Then all was quiet.

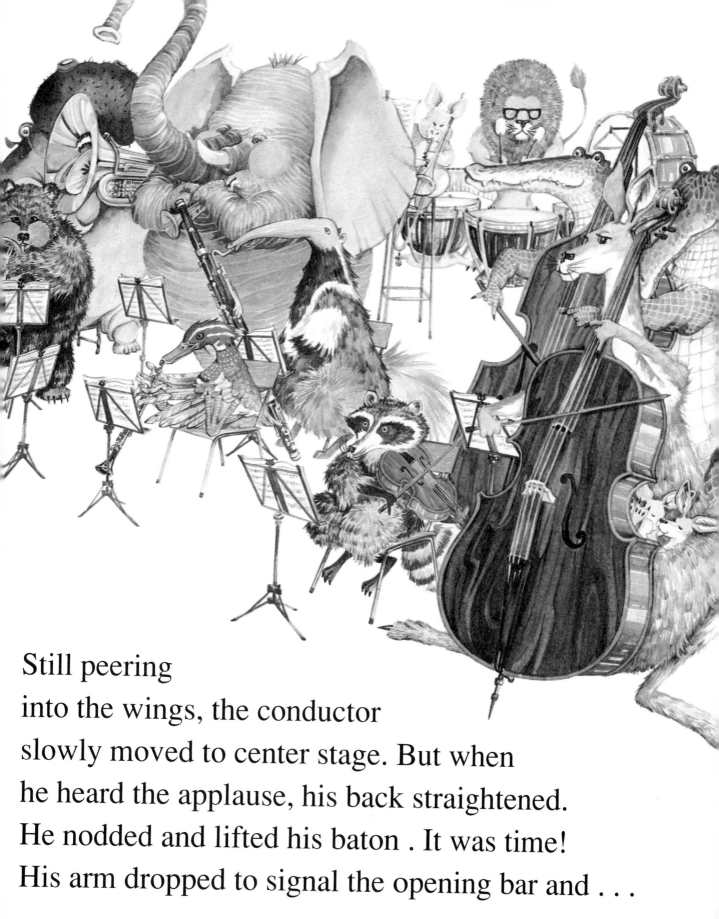

Still peering
into the wings, the conductor
slowly moved to center stage. But when
he heard the applause, his back straightened.
He nodded and lifted his baton . It was time!
His arm dropped to signal the opening bar and . . .

Crash banged his cymbals right on cue!

As the last strains faded away,
clapping and bravos rang from all sides.
The conductor smiled widely and bowed low,
then gestured to the orchestra.
They rose, beaming.

The curtain opened and closed three times
but still the crowd called for Crash,
and the final cheers were for him alone.
He was the star of the show!

"Same time tomorrow?"
muttered the conductor.